Di chu

the little panda

For Holly

ORCHARD BOOKS
96 Leonard Street, London, EC2A 4XD
Orchard Books Australia
Unit 31, 56 O'Riordan Street, Alexandria, NSW 2015
ISBN 1 84121 747 6
First published in Great Britain in 2001
© John Butler 2001
The right of John Butler to be identified as the author and
illustrator of this Work has been asserted by him in
accordance with the Copyright, Designs and Patents Act 1988.
A CIP catalogue record for this book is available from the British Library.
Printed in Hong Kong/China

Pi-shu

the little panda

John Butler

 ORCHARD BOOKS

On the slopes of Misty Mountain, in central China, lay a mother panda cuddling her tiny baby. Hidden in the hollow trunk of an old tree, she washed him, and fed him with her warm milk as he snuggled happily into her thick, soft fur. His name was Pi-shu, and he was no bigger than one of the patches around his mother's eyes.

He was born with a little pink tail which would
slowly disappear as he grew. His mother Fei-Fei
thought he was the most beautiful baby
panda she had ever seen.

Pi-shu was never left alone
for long, and Fei-Fei would
often cradle him gently
in her strong arms.

As Pi-shu grew into a little furry bundle, Fei-Fei would carry him around on her back. At six months he could walk on his own, and he started to copy his mother, chewing on bamboo. Pi-shu liked the rough taste in his mouth. In another three months he would stop taking her milk.

By his first birthday Pi-shu
was strong and adventurous.
Everywhere he looked there
were things to play with...

trees to climb...

frogs that jumped
when he sniffed them...

bamboo rats that played hide-and-seek in and out of their burrows.

One day, as early winter storms gathered over the mountains, Pi-shu saw a troop of golden monkeys high in the treetops. He followed them as they leapt gracefully from tree to tree.

Pi-shu trotted after the monkeys as fast as he could. He had never been so far down the mountainside before, and as he pushed through some thick ferns he smelt something that made him wary. There was a chopping noise he didn't like, and loud voices that were strange to him.

Pi-shu froze as a huge crash shook the ground under his feet.
A tree had fallen. Peering out from the ferns he saw, to his
amazement, he was at the very edge of the forest. The trees had
all been stripped away to grow crops of rice and corn, and men
were chopping down more trees to burn on their winter fires.
Frightened, Pi-shu turned and ran back to find his mother.

Pi-shu chased through the undergrowth, scared he might be lost. He came to a small clearing in the forest, and nearly ran into a takin, grazing with her baby. They stared at each other in surprise before Pi-shu scampered on, still looking for his mother.

When Pi-shu found Fei-Fei, she could see that he was very afraid. She knew that this part of the forest wasn't safe any more. It was time to leave.

Early next morning Pi-shu and Fei-Fei set off, climbing higher and higher until they reached a misty plateau. Their oily fur kept them warm, but it was hard work clambering over the slippery rocks, especially for little Pi-shu.

With nothing to eat, and the first snows falling, Pi-shu and Fei-Fei crossed the high alpine meadow into the next valley, where they found a small clump of bamboo. This valley looked quiet and peaceful, and resting against a cold, hard rock, they slept as best they could.

They awoke next day to a blanket of
snow. Slowly they descended the steep
slope into the valley, feeding on
bamboo as they came to it.

It was evening when Pi-shu and Fei-Fei reached the valley floor and found a clear mountain stream near a lush grove of bamboo. They ate their fill, and settled into a contented sleep as darkness fell. Pi-shu would want to find a place of his own to live one day, and climb his own mountains, but right now he didn't want to change a thing, not for all the bamboo in China.

Panda facts

Pi-shu is an ancient Chinese name for pandas, meaning 'brave'. Giant pandas spend most of their time on their own, and are found in mountainous regions in central China. Panda babies are usually born as twins and are only 10 cm long at birth. Sadly, the mother normally abandons the weakest, but takes great care of the stronger one.

A Giant panda eats about 15 kg of bamboo a day to keep alive, though some have been recorded eating 40 kg or more, which is nearly half their bodyweight. Pandas eat different types of bamboo depending on the time of year, mainly arrow bamboo in winter and umbrella bamboo in summer.

Some experts say that pandas are more closely related to raccoons than bears, but nobody knows why they have such unusual markings. Possibly it is to see and communicate with each other in the thick forest.

Giant pandas are endangered because people are using or destroying their habitat, so they have less space and less food available. There are only about one thousand pandas left in the wild.